THE BOY WHO TURNED OVER A NEW LEAF

THE BOOKWORM
WHO TURNED
OVER A NEW LEAF

DON CONROY

POOLBEG

FOR CHILDREN

Published 1998 by
Poolbeg Press Ltd
123 Baldoyle Industrial Estate
Dublin 13, Ireland

Reprinted December 1998

The Arts Council
An Chomhairle Ealaíon

A catalogue record for this book is available from the British Library.

ISBN 1 85371 818 1

Illustrations by Don Conroy
Cover design by Poolbeg Group Services Ltd
Set by Poolbeg Group Services Ltd in Times 15/21.5
Printed by The Guernsey Press Ltd,
Vale, Guernsey, Channel Islands.

About the Author

Don Conroy is a well-known writer of children's fiction, television personality and an enthusiastic observer of wildlife. He sketches animals and birds native to Ireland and is one of Ireland's best-loved writers and illustrators for children. *The Anaconda from Drumcondra* and *Elephant at the Door* are also available in this series.

Also in this series

The Anaconda from Drumcondra
Elephant at the Door

Published by Poolbeg

To Richard

Chapter 1

A New Leaf

"Get out and stay out!" yelled an angry librarian as he threw the book out of a window.

A blackbird gave out a loud alarm call as he watched the book hurtle through the air. The book split open and pages danced briefly in the air before falling to the ground. Some of the leaves landed in a cherry tree where the blackbird was sitting.

"They've no appreciation of good music around here," the blackbird grumbled as he flew off to a nearby park.

The book finally came to rest in a large yellow skip, full to the brim with old broken timbers, plaster, wallpaper and a three-legged chair. The book in question was a hardback copy of Charles Dickens' *Great Expectations*. It lay in a sorry state, the tattered cover hanging off and brown spots called "foxing marks" across most of the remaining pages.

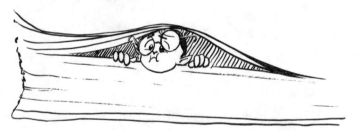

Suddenly, the pages began to rustle and Clive the bookworm emerged from between a few leaves. "What the Dickens!"

he mumbled to himself, feeling rather dizzy from his unexpected flight. "Oh, dear," he sighed, looking at pages of the book strewn about. "That was such a good read. I was over halfway through it . . ."

Clive had realised something was happening to the old library when the builders moved in and started pulling up floorboards and drilling large holes in the ceiling. But to be thrown out of one's home without as much as an apology . . . He had been told by his old friend Wilfred that he would have a long shelf-life there.

Clive expected to have gone through all the Dickens volumes by Christmas. "Nobody reads Dickens now," he was assured, "unless they're locked up in prison or on a desert island. So you won't be disturbed."

Clive couldn't understand why not. Dickens was, he had discovered, a darn good read! Wordy, perhaps, but very exciting. Clive cleaned the dust off his glasses and looked at the book. The ending was missing.

"I hate that," he grumbled. "Being interrupted in the middle of a good read . . ." He climbed up on to a bed spring and yelled at the library, hoping the librarian would hear: "I bet you wouldn't do that to a first edition!"

As if in reply, another book shot through the air, landing on top of Clive, knocking him down and nearly flattening him.

"Ouch!" he yelled as he tried to crawl out from under the book. It was a dictionary and very heavy.

"Every cloud has a silver lining," his friend Wilfred used to say. Clive certainly hoped so. Suddenly, a flock of starlings alighted on the ground in search of any scraps or insects that might have been disturbed by the building work. Some of the cheeky starlings hopped up on to the skip and probed about, pulling at the leaves of paper and the rubble. One found a piece of yesterday's lunch that a workman had discarded.

Clive watched a tug-of-war between two starlings as one tried to pull a rasher rind from the other. Some of the other starlings spied a sandwich at the base of the skip. They swarmed down like flies, stabbing and pulling the sandwich apart. Some got the cheese, others the bread. The sound of machines starting up sent the starlings flying to cover.

Clive decided to lie low until things quietened down. He read a page of words beginning with *del*, memorising every word and its meaning. Clive prided himself on his photographic memory. When he had finished, he polished off the whole page for lunch. He noticed as he was chewing the word *delicious* that it tasted simply wonderful. He remembered Wilfred remarking on this as he made his way through an entire dictionary one winter.

Other bookworms didn't believe him. Words like *delightful*, *tasty* and *splendid* all had exceptional flavour, but words like *putrid*, *horrible* and *vile* always tasted awful. Wilfred even claimed they gave him indigestion. The other bookworms always laughed and sneered at his claims.

"I suppose," Clive pondered, "if one is used to eating trashy novels, one's taste buds are affected." Wilfred had advised Clive to stick to quality books – the classics, especially Shakespeare. "If you must eat the words of modern writers, make sure they are prize-winners. These are main meal books, the others are merely dessert." Clive remembered, with a smile, that Wilfred had said it was okay to read and devour the occasional children's book – as a special treat.

After his meal, Clive stretched out on an old cushion and decided to have a nap. He found this aided his digestion. He was most comfortable, lying there with the book cover hiding him from any prying eyes, such as those of birds and cats. Before he knew it, he'd drifted into a lovely sleep; and what a wonderful dream he had! He dreamed he was in a land where mountains were made of books and roads were paved with rice paper.

Chapter 2

In the Dumps

Suddenly Clive felt a chilly wind. He opened his eyes to discover the book had blown away. A full moon hung low in the night sky. Clive didn't realise he had slept for so long. On looking around, everything appeared different to him. There was no library to be seen; even the skip he had fallen into was gone. Then he realised he was in the city dump. He couldn't understand how he had slept through all the disturbance. Maybe he shouldn't eat full pages in future. He should stick to half pages, that way he wouldn't sleep for so long.

Well, this was a fine mess he was in, kicked out of his home and literally dumped into a rubbish tip. He heard a loud shriek which nearly made him faint with fright. What could have made such a bloodcurdling noise? he wondered.

Then he saw a beautiful barn owl flying low over the dump. He wondered if he could convince this big bird to give him a lift back to the city. He watched the owl circling before alighting on a nearby fence post.

"Excuse me, Miss Owl . . . "

The barn owl swivelled her head to see where the voice had come from. Although the owl had excellent eyesight, she could not see who was calling.

"Over here," said Clive. The owl flapped over to locate where the voice was coming from, then she spied the bookworm. The owl blinked at Clive, who blinked back, thinking this must be the way owls greet each other. "Good evening," said Clive. "I  wonder, could you help me? I'm in a spot of bother. You see, I have been accidentally removed from the city and I need to get back there. Oh, forgive me, I never introduced myself. I'm Clive. I'm a bookworm."

"Pleased to meet you," said the owl. "My name is Snowdrop."

"Do you read much?" Clive asked.

"Read?" said the owl. "You mean, read the signs – whether it's going to be stormy or cold, or when spring will arrive . . . is that what you mean?"

"Well, not exactly; I mean to read a book."

"I'm afraid not," said the owl.

Clive cleaned his glasses. "Forgive me," he said, a little embarrassed. "Because I'm a bookworm, I assume all creatures read. Of course, some of my own kind never read a word; they simply think paper is mere food. You know, you are mentioned in a lot of books," said Clive brightly.

"I am?" said Snowdrop.

"Oh, yes," said the bookworm. "You are nearly always mentioned in wildlife books . . . and famous writers like William Shakespeare mention you."

The owl seemed pleased and puffed up

12

her feathers. "How extraordinary. Tell me, what do they say?"

"Oh, lots of things," said Clive. "'Tu-whit, tu-who-a merry note, while greasy Joan doth keel the pot.'"

The owl looked at the bookworm blankly. "I don't 'who'," she said.

"Oh, well, that referred to a tawny owl," Clive said. He scratched his head with the tip of his tail. "I've got it!" He took a deep breath. "'It was the owl that shrieked, the fatal bellman.' Now that's a barn owl all right," said Clive proudly.

The owl seemed pleased. Clive added. "There are so many things written about the wise old owl . . . stories, poems, legends . . ."

"'Old'?" said the owl.

"Figure of speech," said Clive quickly. "In ancient Greece the owl was considered the wisest of birds."

"Well, then, I would be delighted to give you a lift to the city," said Snowdrop.

Clive wriggled up along her tail and made his way up to the owl's shoulders, wrapping himself around her neck. He felt safe and secure, nestled in her soft feathers. "All aboard!" he shouted.

With one swish of her wings they were airborne, flying across the starry sky.

"Yippee!" yelled Clive, unable to conceal his excitement.

The owl swooped low over a river, then glided across a meadow. A large chestnut tree stood tall in the middle of a field. Clive thought they were going to crash into it. He closed his eyes, but just before they reached the outer branches the owl ascended high into the sky and flew over its crown.

"That was exciting," shouted Clive, as he opened one eye to see if all was well. The outskirts of the city loomed large ahead.

"Nearly there," said Snowdrop, as she flapped over the factories and the rows and rows of houses. The barn owl alighted on a tall statue in the centre of the city. "We're here," she said, gently lifting Clive from her back with her bill and placing him on the head of the statue.

"I would like to thank you most sincerely," said Clive. "You've saved me from a very long crawl, and I must add that I really enjoyed the flight."

"Would you prefer to be placed on the ground?" the owl asked.

"We're here," she said, gently lifting Clive from her back with her bill and placing him on the head of the statue.

"It's wonderful up here," said Clive as he surveyed the city at night with all its bright flashing lights. "I can see the world from the ground anytime."

"Well, I must be away," said Snowdrop. "I hope you find a new home with lots of books to enjoy."

Clive thanked the owl for her kindness and watched her silently flap away back to the countryside. "There's a lot to be said for having wings," he remarked to himself, as he sat there looking up at the starry night. "The world looks so different from this height. I truly have a bird'seye view of the city." He smiled as he thought of the humans hurrying about below. They look just like ants, always busying themselves. Clive yawned. All this fresh air was making him sleepy again. He settled himself in the ear of the statue which sheltered him from the chilly breeze. Soon he was fast asleep.

Chapter 3

New Friends, New Home

Clive awoke to the sound of a woodpigeon cooing from a plane tree. Soon the roar of the city traffic drowned out its call. "Time to get up," he said to himself. He then became aware of how far down he would have to crawl to reach the pavement. He wondered if he should try to jump down in stages. He decided to take the plunge. He closed his eyes and jumped. "Phew, that wasn't too difficult," he said to himself with a sigh of relief when he'd landed.

When he opened his eyes and looked around, he realised that he had landed on the extended hand of the statue.

"I still have a long way to go," he sighed. He mustered up his courage and jumped again. This time he could feel the wind rushing past him as he cut through the air. He opened one eye and saw the ground coming towards him fast.

Suddenly, a swallow flew towards him with its mouth opened wide. Clive knew this meant trouble. Luckily for him, this early visitor from Africa was more interested in a cloud of midges which he'd just passed through.

Opening both eyes, Clive could see he was plummeting to the ground. It looked awfully hard. At times like this, he would be most grateful for some brakes. At least he had no bones that would break on impact. With any luck he'd come away with only a few bruises to show for his reckless behaviour. He had watched spiders hurling themselves from tall buildings or trees, but they always managed to produce silken bungee cords just in the nick of time.

Suddenly Clive landed on something soft. No one was more surprised than he was. They must be making concrete softer, he guessed, for he hadn't the slightest bump or bruise on his body. Although

he had landed, he still felt like he was moving. "How strange," he thought, until he realised that he had landed on a hat and that below the hat was a gentleman who was walking very quickly.

Clive decided to stay put. Soon the man would remove the hat, then he could climb off. He was rather pleased with himself for getting all these different lifts. Crawling could become a bit of a bore sometimes, and there were times when it was downright dangerous, what with all those big feet walking up and down the footpaths. Some people, he noticed, had very big feet indeed.

It was worse, of course, when someone spotted him. They would shriek loudly and proceed deliberately to try to step on him, which wasn't very friendly. How would they feel if a giant bug tried to step on them? They wouldn't like it one bit. No, he decided, he would stay up here as long as he could.

The man turned the corner of the main street and entered a small café.

"Good morning, Jack," said the owner. "Same as usual?"

"Yes," said the man. "Can you put a few mushrooms on the side?" He turned and sat down, removing his hat and placing it on the table. He pulled out the daily paper and a pen and proceeded to do the crossword.

Clive sneaked himself off the hat and hid himself among the red carnations in a vase on the table. A big breakfast arrived for the man.

"Ah, thanks, Bernard. Just the way I like it, fried bread and all."

Clive became very hungry watching the man tuck into his hearty breakfast. He slipped down the stamen of the flower and then slid down the vase. He decided to have his breakfast too and gobbled up the red paper napkin.

A woman sitting at the opposite table watched as the napkin began slowly to disappear. She could not believe her eyes. She took off her glasses and cleaned them, peering over at the table in disbelief as another red napkin began to disappear.

"How did you do that?" she asked Jack as he finished his breakfast.

"Quite easily, madam. I get up at seven every morning, go for a brisk walk, buy the paper and, by the time I arrive here, I'm ravenous." He picked up a napkin and wiped his mouth. Then he put it back on his plate.

"Do it again," she asked. He stared at her blankly.

"Well, if you insist." He picked up the napkin and wiped his mouth again. "Make it disappear," she insisted.

"Madam, the only thing I can make disappear is my breakfast," he declared, lifting up his empty plate. "Which, you can see, I have already done."

Clive couldn't resist eating that napkin as well.

The woman watched as the napkin vanished in front of her eyes. "You're some magician," she said, patting him on the shoulder as she left.

"You do get some odd customers around here," Jack remarked to the owner. Then he looked down at his plate and the napkin was gone. He wondered what could have happened to the napkin. It had been there a minute ago. He checked to see if it had fallen under the table. It must have been that woman . . . she'd picked it up as a joke.

He proceeded to work on his crossword. Clive wriggled up on his shoulder to take a look, for he was very interested in general knowledge quizzes. He'd picked up the interest from Wilfred: his mentor, as he liked to call himself.

"Twins of the eternal city," Jack said loudly, hoping he would get a prompt from Bernard, the owner. Bernard scratched his head and pulled at his chin.

Then a voice sounded. "Romulus and Remus."

"Thanks, Bernard," said Jack as he wrote down the answer. "Here are a few more,

Bernard. What year did the Romans first invade Britain?"

"Well, the first time was 55 BC," said Clive.

"Hold on for a minute, Bernard, that could be right."

"*Could* be?" said Clive. "It is!"

"What year was Galileo Galilei born?"

Bernard poured himself a cup of coffee, put two heaped spoons of sugar in it and began to stir furiously to give the impression he was concentrating hard. "Galileo was born in 1564 and died in 1642."

"Great stuff," said Jack. "We're flying through this crossword. This one might be tough, Bernard. How long did it take to build the Taj Mahal?"

"Twenty-two years," said Clive. "It involved twenty thousand workers in the construction."

"Here's another one you might know. 'Was this the – something – that launched a thousand ships?'"

Bernard scratched his head again and screwed up his face.

"The face," said Clive. "It's from *Doctor Faustus* by Christopher Marlowe."

"That's it," said Jack. "Bernard, you're a genius. If we keep this up I might actually finish the crossword for a change."

Bernard smiled awkwardly, feeling very confused.

"Start of dinosaur age? Eight letters."

"You have me there," said Bernard.

"Me too," said Jack. "My nephew would probably be able to help if he was here. He's mad about dinosaurs. Has all those books and posters. Eight letters . . ." he pondered and chewed on the top of his pen.

"It's obvious," said Clive. "It's the Triassic period. Started about two hundred and twenty-five million years ago. Did you know these awesome creatures dominated the earth for over a hundred million years?"

"I didn't," mumbled Jack, as he filled in the letters. "That fits, all right." Then, looking suspiciously over his glasses at

Bernard, he said, "I thought you said you didn't know the answer to that question . . . "

"I didn't," said Bernard.

"Well, if you didn't and I didn't, then who gave us the answer?"

"Who? Me, of course!" said Clive.

"Who said that?" Jack asked anxiously looking around the café. A canary chirped in a cage by the window. "Are you teaching that bird to speak?" Jack asked.

"No, he only sings," said Bernard.

"Maybe your wife has been teaching it some words."

"I don't think so," said the owner as the two of them moved over to the birdcage. The canary hopped anxiously from perch to perch as they peered in.

"How long have you had the bird?"

"Only a few months," said Bernard. "My wife's brother bought it for her on her birthday."

"Maybe this bird lived with a professor or a teacher before it was bought for your wife." They heard a small chuckle of laughter. "Did you hear that?" said Jack. "And its beak didn't even move."

"Ask it another question from the crossword," Bernard suggested.

"Good idea!" Jack scanned the remaining questions. "Anteater of Africa!" They watched the canary. It moved to the corner of its cage. "It's thinking," said Jack. "Look." They watched for a few seconds, then the bird hopped to the centre of its cage and began to feed on the seed. "It doesn't know," said Jack.

"Probably lost interest," said Bernard.

"It's an aardvark."

"Yes," said Jack. "That's it."

They asked the canary several more questions and received correct answers.

"Well, that's the first time I've actually completed a crossword," Jack said proudly. Pointing at the canary, he continued, "That bird could make you a fortune."

"Do you think so?" said Bernard.

"I do," said Jack. "Mark my words, if anyone ever uses the expression 'bird-brained' to me, I'll set them straight."

"Surely, if my wife wanted a talking bird she would have got a parrot or a mynah bird, not a canary."

"Listen, Bernard. Only you and I know that canary there did this crossword. I admit I didn't have a clue to the answers to most of those questions."

"Well, I have to tell you, Jack, I didn't give you any clues either. So it has to be the canary."

"I beg to differ," said Clive. "No disrespect to you, dear fellow," he added, looking at the canary. "I admire your singing greatly. But it was I who helped you gentlemen complete the crossword," he said proudly, pushing his glasses up the bridge of his nose.

Jack's and Bernard's heads spun from side to side trying to locate the voice.

"Right here," said Clive. "On your left shoulder."

"Ah! Ah!" said Bernard. "It's a bug." He flicked it with his thumb and index finger, sending Clive shooting across the room. Luckily, he fell in a geranium pot which made for a very soft landing.

"You'd want to watch that," said Jack. "If a health inspector called in, he'd be none too pleased to find bugs crawling on the customers."

"Hold on for a minute, Jack," said the owner. "You know my place is spotless; you must have picked it up on your walk through the park."

"Hold your horses," said Jack, smiling broadly. "Do you realise you just knocked a potential gold mine off my shoulder?"

"You're right," said Bernard.

"Let's try and find it," said Jack.

"Fancy a bug that can talk," said Bernard, as he began to crawl on all fours looking for Clive. Jack also got down on his hands and knees and began to search under cushions and chairs. "Here, buggy wuggy," called Bernard.

"Buggy wuggy?" repeated Jack with a grin.

"Well, if a cat will answer to 'Kitty Kitty', why not a bug to 'buggy wuggy'?" Bernard retorted.

"Gentlemen, I'm over here," said Clive. "And please get up from the floor – you look ridiculous."

Jack and Bernard turned quickly, trying to locate the voice, and crashed their heads together. "Ouch!" yelled the two men.

Clive felt like saying "Serves you right for the way you treated me," but he decided against it.

"You really *can* talk," said Jack as the two men stared down at Clive.

"I pride myself on good diction and a rich vocabulary. I also speak fluent French, German, Italian, Spanish, Latin, Irish and Greek. I have a smattering of Mandarin. I must brush up on my Russian."

"Wow," said Bernard, extending his

finger. Clive knew he wanted him to climb on to it. Clive felt no danger this time so he climbed on to the finger. Bernard carefully carried him over to the counter and took out a magnifying glass which he used to read small print.

"Let me see," said Jack, pulling the magnifying glass from him. "You are rather tiny," said Jack.

"Well, what did you expect?" said Clive indignantly. "I'm a bookworm, not an anaconda!"

"Would you like some breakfast?" Bernard asked.

"I wouldn't say no to a thimble full of freshly-squeezed orange juice and three more of those delicious napkins."

Bernard hurried to get a thimble from another room, then produced a wad of napkins. "Does it matter what colour?" he asked.

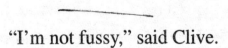

"I'm not fussy," said Clive.

The men poured themselves two large mugs of tea and settled down on stools beside Clive. "First, we'd like to apologise for the way we treated you."

"I should think so," said Clive, adjusting his glasses.

"My name is Jack Black and this is my

friend and the owner of the Honey Pot, Bernard Alwell."

"Delighted to make your acquaintance. I'm Clive the bookworm."

"Where did you come from?" Bernard enquired.

"Well, I've been living in a library all my life, beside Blossom Park. Unfortunately for me and my colleagues, they decided to modernise the library and some of the books were in poor condition."

"I'm not surprised, what with you lot about," said Jack. "Oops, sorry, I meant no offence."

"None taken," said Clive. "Well," he continued, "Between the jigs and the reels, I ended up in the dump on the outskirts of the city. A barn owl gave me a lift here. She knew I'd never go hungry in a city full of paper."

"Have you got a place to stay?" Jack asked.

"Not yet," said Clive, who had given very little thought to the matter.

"You're welcome and come and stay in my place," said Jack. "You see, Bernard couldn't have your kind around where there is food involved . . . oops, I didn't mean that the way it sounded."

"I understand perfectly well," said Clive. He drank down the juice and ate two folded pink napkins. "Mmmm. Delicious," he said with satisfaction.

"Do you know everything?" asked Bernard.

"No one knows *everything*," said Clive. "But I do pride myself on a well-rounded education. I'm mainly self-taught, though I did have a dear friend called Wilfred who started me off on a good education. Learning, he said, was to bring out the best in one."

"Too true," said Jack, agreeing with him. Bernard nodded as well.

"You see," said Clive, "most of my kind simply graze, never reading a line. What a waste, don't you agree?"

"Oh, yes," said Bernard. "It should be made compulsory for a bookworm eating a book to read it as well."

"Well, let's not be fanatical either," said Clive. "Reading is a pleasurable pastime, to be encouraged rather than forced."

Jack elbowed Bernard. "He's right, there's nothing worse than intolerant fanatics."

"I just meant . . ."

"We understand," said Jack, interrupting Bernard. "Please continue," he said warmly.

"Well, my dear friend and mentor, Wilfred, was accidentally packed off one night in a hard-bound edition of Milton's

Paradise Lost. It was said the books were being sent to London for restoration along with Shakespeare's complete works and books by Edmund Spenser, Andrew Marvell and Samuel Johnson. You're familiar with their works?" Clive asked.

"Not exactly . . ." said Jack.

"Me neither," said Bernard.

"I keep forgetting . . . since I was brought up in a library, I assume everyone is familiar with all the different writers."

"Did you ever find out what happened to Wilfred?" Jack enquired.

"I'm afraid not," Clive sighed.

Trying to change the subject, Jack asked, "Would you fancy going to a table quiz? We could certainly do with your help."

"It's in aid of the local Primary School," Bernard added.

"Sounds fun," said Clive.

"Wonderful," said Jack. "Then we'd better be on our way."

"Hold it," said Bernard. "I have just the thing for you to travel in." He hurried back to the kitchen. They could hear drawers opening and closing and things being lifted in and out. "Got it!" shouted Bernard from the other room. Then he appeared with a small silver object. He flicked the lid open, tore off a piece of tissue and lined the inside of the box. "Here is your new bed and travel case," he beamed proudly.

"It's lovely," said Clive. "An eighteenth-century French snuffbox! You shouldn't have."

"Well done," said Jack.

"Sorry there's no snuff in it," Bernard winked.

"Oh, I wouldn't touch the stuff," said Clive.

The two men laughed loudly. Jack

placed Clive carefully in the box and clipped it shut, then placed it in his top pocket. "All right there, Clive?" he said, tapping his jacket pocket.

"Fine, thank you," Clive answered.

"See you lads tonight," said Bernard, as he watched them leave through the front door. Jack walked down the road with a spring in his step, greeting everyone he passed. Clive was glad he'd found such cheerful company. He found the snuffbox exceedingly comfortable; a little warm perhaps, but that was a small complaint.

Chapter 4

Bright Sparks!

That evening, Jack and Bernard entered the Winning Post. Jack rubbed his hands with glee, for two tables away sat the headmaster, the solicitor, the accountant and the librarian. They always teamed up together and always came first in these competitions.

"Hope you brought your lucky rabbit's foot," said the accountant to Jack. "You'll need it." The rest of his team laughed loudly.

"I've something much better," Jack chuckled back at them.

Matt Sweeney, the compère and c o m e d i a n , appeared on the makeshift stage and grabbed the

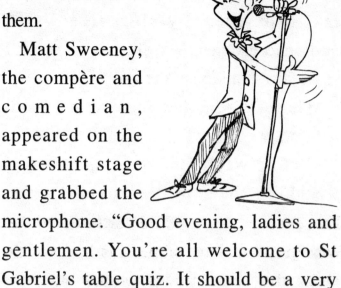

microphone. "Good evening, ladies and gentlemen. You're all welcome to St Gabriel's table quiz. It should be a very exciting evening and it's for a good cause. I hope you all have been sharpening your wits and that you brought your brains with you."

The crowd shouted a few heckles. He pointed at one man drinking a pint. "You remind me of that wall over there . . . it's plastered, too! No, seriously, folks, I had to

43

hurry here to be on time. I ran behind the 46A and saved myself eighty pence. Someone told me I should have run after a taxi and saved myself a fiver." The audience groaned. "Well, if you think I stink you should visit the toilet."

"Get off!" the audience yelled good-naturedly.

"Before we get the quiz under way, I would like you to put your hands together and give a big round of applause to my next guest, making her first appearance on stage tonight. Well, it's not much of a stage, but she's a wonderful singer. Please welcome, from Cherrywood Drive, Jodie Whelan."

"I didn't know your niece was a singer," said Jack to Bernard.

"There's lots you don't know," Bernard retorted.

"Excuse me," said Clive. "I'd like to see

44

the singer." Jack took out the snuffbox and opened it on the table.

Just then Bernard's wife hurried in, taking off her coat as she sat down at the table. "Sorry I'm late! I'm glad I'm on time for Jodie. She's a gorgeous singer. Hi, Jack."

"Hello, Rita." She looked at the snuffbox and saw Clive wriggling about trying to get comfortable.

"Is that the maggot you were telling me about?"

"It's a bookworm, Rita."

"Does it bite?"

"Only if you're a paper bag," Jack chuckled.

"You should be up on stage instead of Sweeney," said Bernard.

"Shush," said Rita, as Jodie began to sing.

When she finished to loud applause, Jodie hurried over and joined Rita, Bernard, Jack and Clive.

"You have a voice like an angel," said Clive.

"Thank you, Jack. That's the nicest thing anyone has ever said about my singing."

"It wasn't me," said Jack. "Although I think you're very good indeed."

"Who was it, then?" Jodie wondered.

"It was Clive here." Jack pointed at the snuffbox.

Jodie looked into the box and shrieked. Everyone looked around. Jodie smiled awkwardly at them. Jack quickly closed over the box as a waiter passed by. "Sorry," said Jodie. "But you know I hate creepy-crawlies."

"This is no ordinary worm," said Jack quietly. "It's a

46

highly intelligent one. His name is Clive."

Jodie gently lifted the lid and peered in at the bookworm. "Hi, there," she smiled warmly. "Sorry for screaming at you."

"Don't give it a second thought," said Clive. "I usually have that effect on people."

At last the table quiz got under way. The first question was "What was James Joyce's full name?"

"Who thinks up these questions?" Jodie sighed.

"Jimmy," Bernard muttered.

"No," said Jack, scratching his chin. "That's slang for James."

"Oh, right, silly me," said Bernard.

"Don't look at me," said Rita. "I've never read a word written by the man."

Jack looked over at the accountant and his team. They were busy whispering to each other. Then he looked at Clive, who was curled up and dozing off. He prodded him with his finger.

"Clive, wake up. No time for sleeping now, this is important."

"Oh, sorry," said Clive. "The heat and the smoke are getting to me."

"I'll fix that," said Jack. He placed two fingers into a glass of water, then sprinkled some on Clive's head.

"That's better," said Clive. "I feel refreshed already. What was the question again? Never mind, I remember – James

Augustine Aloysius Joyce, that's his full name."

"Thanks Clive," said Jack as he scribbled down the answer.

"What famous astronomer produced the theory of the expanding universe?"

"Do they think we're all rocket scientists or what?" Rita remarked with frustration.

"Clive," said Jack. "Any ideas?"

"Well, I did spend some time in the science and astronomy shelf . . . now, let me think."

"Bernard, look at the others."

Most of the teams were looking at each other blankly except table four, where the accountant and his team were busy scribbling.

"I remember," said Clive. "It was the American astronomer Edwin Powell Hubble, born in 1889, departed this life in 1953."

"Of course," said Jack. "Sure, didn't they name that telescope they put in space after him."

"We're doing great," said Jodie, "thanks to you." She tapped Clive's box gently.

He began to blush. "Oh, it was nothing."

"It's far from over yet," said Jack with cautionary tones.

"He's right," said Bernard. "Nothing worse than becoming complacent."

"Listen," said Rita. "Here's the next question coming up."

Matt Sweeney took a gulp of water from his glass, wiped his mouth, and read out another question. "Famous French novel made into several films, the most recent being an animated one."

"I know," said Jodie. "It's Victor Hugo's *The Hunchback of Notre Dame*." She beamed broadly.

"Not just a pretty face," said Jack.

"You've competition, Clive," Bernard joked.

"At least we're on the same team," Clive said, smiling at Jodie.

"Who was Spinoza?" Matt Sweeney held up another question. "Don't blame me," said the compère. "I just read the questions, I don't think them up."

"Baruch Spinoza was a Dutch philosopher born in 1632," Clive said with confidence.

"You're a walking encyclopaedia," said Rita.

"Crawling," said Bernard, shaking with laughter.

"What famous American rock singer was born in 1935?"

"Elvis Presley," said Jodie.

"Now that's more like it," said Rita. "Some decent questions."

"What's Cliff Richard's real name?"

"I know!" Rita yelled loudly.

"Shush," said Bernard. "We need to keep the answers to ourselves."

"Harry Roger Webb," she said excitedly, winking at Clive.

Clive cleaned his glasses and said, "I'm afraid I didn't know the last two answers. I must brush up on popular culture."

"Here's one for the ladies," said Matt, finishing his drink as he read the next card. "Who gave the most famous haircut in the world?"

"Delilah gave it to Samson," said Rita proudly.

"I didn't realise you were so versed in the Good Book," said Jack.

"I'm not really," said Rita. "But I saw the film with Hedy Lamarr and Victor Mature. Now he's what you'd call a hunk," she declared.

"Who, me?" smiled Jack.

"No, Victor. He can rescue me anytime."

"Listen, that was another film question," said Jodie. "Turn on your microphone!" she yelled up at Matt.

There was a loud screeching sound. "Can you hear me now?" Matt asked, banging the mouthpiece with his hand and blowing into it.

"Yes, we can hear you," yelled someone before adding, "unfortunately."

This brought a round of laughter from the audience.

"I'll ignore that remark," said Matt before continuing. "Who starred in and directed the film *Braveheart*?"

"Mel Gibson," Jodie whispered. "Now he's *my* kind of hunk."

"I've heard he's quite short," said Rita.

"Will you ladies concentrate," snapped Bernard. "We're ahead of the posse, let's keep it that way!"

"Shush, here we go again," said Rita.

Matt read out another card. "What is a pachyderm?"

Jack looked blankly at Bernard, who looked blankly at Rita who looked blankly at Jodie.

Jodie bent down and smiled at Clive. "Any ideas?"

Clive blushed. "Yes. It means a large, thick-skinned mammal, like an elephant, hippopotamus or rhinoceros."

"Thank you, Clive," she said, tickling

his head with her finger. "You are clever and cute to boot!"

The evening seemed to fly in. Clive continued to answer the questions without any difficulty. Then, at ten o'clock, Matt announced the last question of the evening. "Where is the femoral vein located?"

"That's an awkward question," said Bernard. "I had a fair idea of all the others, but this one has me beaten."

Rita looked at him. "A 'fair idea' of the others," she teased.

"You'd need to be Doctor Kildare to answer that," sighed Jack.

"You mean George Clooney," retorted Jodie. Jack looked blank. "'ER' she added.

"It's located in the thigh," said Clive. "Beside the femoral artery."

"Well done, wormy," said Rita.

There was lots of chatting and comparing of notes, then Matt got up to announce the winner. "Well, this is one for the books," he smiled. "The winning table is number five, with a one hundred per cent score."

Jodie and Rita shrieked with delight. Jack and Bernard clapped each other on the back. The accountant, solicitor, librarian and headmaster looked very annoyed as they got up from their table.

"They've faces like wet weekends," said Rita.

"They can't expect to win every time," said Jodie.

"That's the trouble," said Rita. "They do."

The accountant, Phil Brett, passed by their table. "Surprisingly good win," he remarked.

"It pays to do all these newspaper crosswords," said the solicitor.

"Hope you don't know the person who sets the questions," said the headmaster with a snigger.

"It pays to guess at things," said the librarian.

"What a bunch of sore losers," said Jodie as they passed.

Just then the accountant returned. "I noticed the snuffbox on your table as I passed by." Jack gasped. "My uncle always carried snuff with him in a box just like that."

"Well, it's not his," snapped Rita.

"Oh, I didn't mean to imply anything like that, only to say I enjoy the occasional snort myself. May I?" Before Jack could answer, the accountant picked Clive up and stuck him up his left nostril.

"Aaah!" yelled Jack as he watched Clive disappear up the accountant's long Roman nose.

"Excellent," said the accountant. "Thank you."

Jodie looked at the empty snuffbox. "What should we do?"

Jack, Bernard and Rita all looked helpless. People hurried over and patted them on the back, congratulating them, and Matt the MC presented them with the various prizes they had won – an electric blanket, an alarm clock, a Waterford crystal jug, a set of table-mats, and a gift voucher for £50.

"You know, I would give up all of our prizes to have Clive back," said Jodie. "Hey, I have an idea!" she added. "Quick, follow me." They hurried out of the pub after her.

"Mind these for us," said Bernard, pushing the prizes back at Matt.

Chapter 5

A New Home – But Not For Long

Meanwhile, Clive tried to tickle the hair inside the accountant's nose, so that he would sneeze and hopefully Clive could pop out. Instead, the man stuck his finger up his nose and pushed the bookworm even further up. Now he was truly stuck.

Jodie spotted the accountant on the street and hurried after him. "Hi," she said flirtatiously. "I would just like to thank you and your group for being such good sports. I know your team always wins these quizzes."

"We were a little off form tonight," he replied before adding, "Besides, the prizes weren't as good as they were last year." He began to walk away.

Jodie caught his arm. "I love the springtime, don't you?" she said warmly. Jack, Bernard and Rita followed slowly, sneaking from tree to tree along the avenue. "Let's stroll through the park," suggested Jodie.

"I don't think so," said Phil. "This time of year, all the pollen floating about gives me hay fever."

"Oh, come on," said Jodie. "Don't be an old stick-in-the-mud."

"Very well," he agreed reluctantly. He was pleased that such a pretty girl wanted to walk through the park with him.

"They're heading for the park," said Bernard.

"I can see that," said Jack.

"I wonder why," said Rita. "But, knowing Jodie, she must have a plan."

"Aren't those flowers just beautiful?" said Jodie, sniffing them. "Try," she said waving one in Phil's face.

"No, thank you!" said Phil.

"Look at those red roses just ready to bloom," Jodie said excitedly. "Oh, the scent is just divine!"

"How very nice," said Phil, his eyes beginning to water.

Jodie grabbed hold of an apple blossom branch and sniffed it. "What a delicate scent . . ." she said. Then Jodie let the branch swing back, hitting Phil smack in the face.

61

"Ouch!" he yelled.

"Oh, I'm so sorry," gushed Jodie. "Are you all right?"

"Yes, perfectly . . . " he said, then began to feel a sneeze coming on. "Atishoo!"

Clive shot out of his nose like a bullet from a gun, landing in the centre of a large chrysanthemum.

"Atishoo! Atishoo!"

The others watched as Phil hurried from the park, sneezing all the way home. Jodie couldn't help laughing.

"Well done," said Rita to Jodie. "If all that sneezing didn't shift Clive from that drip's nose, nothing will."

"I'm over here!" shouted Clive, from the centre of the flower-bed.

Jack extended an index finger and Clive climbed on to it.

"Are you all right?" asked Jodie.

"Fine," said Clive. "I'm not used to all this excitement."

"You'll be able to write a book about it before you're done!" laughed Rita.

"Then you can eat it," Bernard added.

They all burst into peals of laughter.

"Let's go for some supper," said Jack. "On me."

"Good idea," said Bernard.

They went to Neptune's fish and chips restaurant.

"Have you ever eaten chips?" Jodie asked Clive.

"No," said Clive. "But I once ate a copy of *Goodbye, Mr Chips*. Does that count?"

They all broke into loud laughter again, which attracted the notice of two men who were sitting quietly in the corner.

"Chips with salt and vinegar . . . nothing like it," said Rita.

"What about a chip butty?" asked Jack.

"Sliced white bread covered with butter, then filled with chips. Now, that's delicious."

They ordered cod, hake, ray and a batter burger with chips. Clive was given a saucer with several chips on it.

"Enjoy," said Jodie.

"Why are they talking to a saucer?" said one of the men watching from the corner.

"How should I know, Dino? Maybe they think it's a UFO," he sniggered.

"Look, Charlie," said Dino. "There were chips on the saucer and they have disappeared. Look for yourself, I'm not kidding." They watched as Jodie placed more chips on the saucer and they slowly vanished.

"See," said Dino.

"That's amazing," said Charlie. "It must be some kind of trick."

"See, they're all looking at the saucer and talking to it."

"No one talks to saucers," snapped Charlie. "There must be something on it."

"I can't see anything," said Dino. He got up and walked towards the toilet, throwing a glance at the saucer. In a moment he was back with his pal Charlie.

"Well?" asked Charlie. "See anything?"

"You wouldn't believe it," said Dino with amazement. He sat down, took out his handkerchief and wiped his brow.

"What wouldn't I believe?" said Charlie, annoyed.

"There's a creepy-crawly bug type

thing in the saucer. It wears glasses and talks."

"You're nuts," said Charlie.

"Go and have a look if you don't believe me," Dino retorted.

"We want to thank you, Clive," said Jack. "We would never have won the table quiz without your help."

"Or finished the crossword," Bernard added.

"It's I who should thank you," said Clive. "I thoroughly enjoyed the evening and the company was splendid."

"I think you'll try chips again," said Rita, laughing.

"Indeed I will," said Clive.

Dino and Charlie watched the four friends leave the restaurant. Then they stood up and followed close behind. After

Jack had said his good-byes to Rita, Bernard and Jodie, he turned to head for his apartment which was in the basement of a fine Georgian house.

As he got ready for bed he placed Clive and his snuffbox on a shelf beside his bed.

"Would you like some supper?" Jack asked.

"No thank you," said Clive. "I'm quite full." Then, looking at a pile of stamps torn from envelopes, Clive piped up: "Mind if I snack on one?"

"Sure," said Jack. "Only I like to keep the ones with the birds and animals. Here, this is a common one, you can eat this."

Outside in the darkness, Dino and Charlie were peering in, watching Clive eating the stamp under a bedroom lamp. "Did you ever see anything like it?" Dino whispered.

*Outside in the darkness, Dino and Charlie
were peering in, watching Clive.*

"That bug is going to make us a bit of money," said Charlie. "But first we have to get our hands on it. When the old geezer is asleep, you break in and take the snuffbox and the bug."

"Why me?" asked Dino. "Why do I always have to do the dirty work?"

"Listen, Dino, I'm the ideas man, you're the action man, right?"

"Right," grumbled Dino.

"Besides, I'll be busy keeping a lookout," said Charlie.

"Try me out on a few questions," said Clive, licking his lips which were a little sticky from the glue on the back of the stamp.

Jack took down an encyclopaedia, put on his glasses and climbed into bed. "Comfortable?" asked Clive.

"Snug as a bug in a rug," said Jack. "If you'll pardon the expression. Okay," he said, flicking through the pages. "When was the Korean War?"

"1950 – 1953," said Clive.

"Spot on," said Jack. "What nationality was the philosopher, Kant?"

"German."

"Berkeley?"

"Irish."

"Marx?"

"German."

"Boy, you sure know your philosophers," Jack remarked. "Who won the *Tour de France* 1987?"

"Stephen Roche."

"Name eight of the world's heavyweight boxing champions?"

"In any particular order?" Clive enquired.

"I'm waiting . . . " Jack smiled.

"John L Sullivan, 1882-92. Jack Dempsey 1919-26. Joe Louis 1937-49. Oh,

I forgot Jim Corbett. There was Rocky Marciano, Muhammad Ali – he had the title three times 1964–67, 74–78, 78–79 – then there was Larry Holmes and, after that, Mike Tyson."

"I'm impressed," said Jack. "You're a genius!"

"Not really," said Clive, yawning. "But I do have a photographic memory."

Jack yawned. "Here are a couple more, then I think we should call it a night. How long were the Beatles together?"

"1960–1970."

"What is an operetta?"

"A light opera which may use spoken dialogue."

"What does NASA stand for?"

"National Aeronautics and Space Administration."

"Last one. What planet is the closest to our sun?"

"Mercury, then Venus, Earth, Mars, Jupiter, Saturn, Uranus, Neptune then Pluto. Am I right?" asked Clive.

All he could hear was loud snoring.

"I suppose I was showing off a bit," Clive scolded himself, pulling over the lid of the snuffbox and settling down to sleep. Suddenly he heard the sound of a door being forced open. He tried to open the lid of his snuffbox but found it closed tightly.

Clive called to Jack to wake up, but Jack couldn't hear him through the closed lid of the snuffbox. All Clive could hear was heavy snoring. Then he heard a gruff voice whispering. He was aware of being moved from his shelf and the smell of tobacco and the sound of a fast-beating heart made him realise he'd been slipped into a pocket. Then he heard the sound of a door closing and footsteps running down the road. Clive was becoming very alarmed. He knew something was up.

The two men hurried into a pub, both panting heavily.

"Two pints of the black stuff; my throat feels like sandpaper," said Charlie to the barman. The barman frowned as it was near closing time but got them anyway.

Dino pulled the snuffbox out of his pocket, flicked open the lid, and peered in at Clive.

"Ugly little mite," he said.

"Hiya, squirmy," said Charlie.

"The name is Clive. I'm a bookworm.

What is the meaning of this abduction from my residence?"

"Fancy talker, isn't he?" said Dino. "Listen, Clive, let me explain. We have you . . ."

"Against my will," Clive interrupted.

"Listen," said Charlie with menace in his voice. "You do what we tell you and everything will be fine. If you don't . . . " he raised a dirty thumb . . . "I'll squash you like a bug! Get my drift?"

"All too clearly . . ." Clive stammered.

Chapter 6

Big Ed

The two men finished their pints, clapped shut the lid on Clive's snuffbox and headed out the door.

"What's the rush?" asked Dino. "I could have done with another pint."

"We're going to see Big Ed. He'll pay good money for this little squirt."

The two men hailed a taxi and Clive found himself listening to the rumble of an engine before they finally arrived at an Italian *bistro*. Charlie and Dino hurried inside. They were stopped halfway across the restaurant by two big, tall men wearing dark glasses.

"Where do you two think you're going?"

"To see Big Ed," said Charlie nervously.

"No one disturbs Big Ed while he's eating."

"It's very important," Dino pleaded.

"He'll be pleased to see us," Charlie added.

One of the men went over to where Big

Ed sat finishing his dessert of banoffi. The man whispered something in his ear. Big Ed looked over at Dino and Charlie, then took out a large Havana cigar and lit it. After blowing a few smoke rings and examining the cigar, he beckoned the two men over.

They took off their hats and stood there trembling. "Hi, Big Ed."

"Don't you guys owe me money?" His face grew stern.

"No," said Dino. "Not us. We're Charlie and Dino. But we do have something we think you'll want to buy."

"I've got everything I want," said Big Ed, blowing smoke into their faces. They started to cough.

"Nice cigars," said Charlie nervously.

"Let's see what you're selling." Big Ed licked his dessert spoon, then sipped his coffee.

Charlie flexed his hands like a magician

and carefully produced the snuffbox from the top pocket of Dino's jacket, flicked open the lid, then carefully placed it on the white tablecloth facing Big Ed.

Big Ed stared at the silver object, then stated to chew the end of his cigar. "What do I want with a snuffbox? I assume that's what it is."

"It's not the snuffbox," said Charlie, becoming braver. "It's what's in it."

Big Ed put his face up close to the box. "Aaah, it's a horrible little slug!" He recoiled in his chair.

"I'm not a slug, snail, bug or insect. I'm a bookworm." The cigar fell from Big Ed's thick lips and landed in his coffee.

"That thing spoke," he said in disbelief. Charlie and Dino grinned at him.

"Oh yes, and he's clever, too," said Dino.

One of Big Ed's bodyguards put another cigar in Big Ed's mouth and lit it for him. He pulled out his wallet that was stuffed with money. "How much for the bug?" Big Ed asked, spreading hundred-pound notes out on the table.

Charlie and Dino's eyes opened wide at the sight of all the money. "Well," said Charlie, loosening his tie. "It's a very rare bug. You can't go into a shop and buy one."

"How about five hundred?" said Big Ed. "I'm feeling generous tonight."

"That should do nicely," said Charlie,

scooping up the money. Dino watched Charlie slip the money into a pocket and Charlie nodded, indicating he'd get his cut later.

"Quick, get me a paper," ordered Big Ed and one of his bodyguards hurried away, returning almost immediately with that day's newspaper. Big Ed opened it at the sports section. He fingered the racing page, then asked Clive to tell him which horse would win at Aintree the next day.

"Excuse me, Mr Ed," said Clive.

"Don't call me Mr Ed," said Big Ed. "That was the name of a horse." Everyone laughed nervously. "Just call me Big Ed, like everyone else."

"Well, er, Big Ed, I would like to inform you that I'm not a soothsayer."

"A what?" said Big Ed.

One of the bodyguards bent over and stared at Clive. "You better show a bit of respect to Big Ed or you'll wind up like a piece of chewing-gum on the pavement. Squashed!"

Clive took off his glasses and cleaned them, before continuing nervously, "What I mean, Big Edward, er, Ed, is that I cannot see into the future. I'm not a prophet or a seer. But I will study the names of the horses and suggest which, in my humble opinion, you should bet on."

"That suits me fine," said Big Ed. Then, looking at Charlie and Dino, he asked, "Why don't you guys come and work for me, taking care of Clive here? You could make sure no magpie makes a meal of him, or nobody flushes him down the toilet. Ha! Ha!" This brought sniggers from the bodyguards.

Charlie and Dino were given cigars. They sat there puffing and coughing.

"Havana," said Big Ed. "Only the best for my friends."

Meanwhile, there was nothing for it but to go along with the situation he found himself in. So Clive began studying the sports page of the newspaper.

"I think Fat Boy," said Clive.

One of the bodyguards picked up a fork and held it over Clive. "What did I tell you about respect? The boss isn't fat, he's only nineteen stone."

"I meant the horse," stuttered Clive anxiously.

"You think I should bet on Fat Boy?" asked Big Ed, blowing blue smoke rings into his face. "I hope you're right, for your sake," he grinned.

Clive spent a sleepless night in Big Ed's mansion. What if the horse lost? Big Ed said he was going to place a very large bet on it. He began to think of Jack, Bernard, Rita and especially Jodie. He hoped they wouldn't be worrying about him. He certainly missed their company. The last thing he wanted was to be in the company of Big Ed and his shady companions.

The next morning Clive paced up and down a walnut tabletop, unable to eat the old newspaper left for him. When would the race be run? he wondered. Early in the afternoon, Charlie and Dino hurried into the large drawing-room. "Big Ed is very happy with you." Charlie pointed at Clive. "The horse came in at seven to one, and he had placed a bet to win of seven thousand pounds."

Clive was relieved and began to feel his appetite returning. Suddenly Big Ed burst into the room. He was wearing a fedora and a crombie coat draped over his shoulders. "Clive!" he bellowed. "My favourite bug. You've done me proud. Tonight we celebrate my winnings. I've ordered my tailor to make a pin-striped suit for you. You've got to look like a winner, Clive. Dress sharp, and you're halfway there."

When the tailor arrived he asked where his client was.

"Over there," said Big Ed who had moved Clive off the table, gesturing towards the sofa. The tailor looked over at the large sofa but could see no one sitting on it. He looked blankly at Big Ed. "Put on your glasses," snapped Big Ed.

"Good afternoon," said Clive. "You won't need much material for me."

The others laughed loudly. With

trembling hands, the tailor measured Clive for his suit. There were hoots of laughter from Big Ed, his bodyguards, Charlie and Dino.

That evening they sat in Donatello's restaurant. "You're looking very smart," said Big Ed to Clive.

"Thank you," said Clive glumly.

"I've brought you some interesting books to eat. I know you're a very learned chap. These books were gathering dust in my library."

"*War and Peace* by Leo Tolstoy," said Clive, reading the covers. "*Heart of Darkness* by Joseph Conrad."

"And for dessert," smiled Big Ed, *The Collected Fairy Tales* by the brothers Grimm."

"How splendid!" said Clive brightly. "I'm really going to enjoy this meal."

Chapter 7

Lonely Mansions

Weeks passed.

Clive became very popular with Big Ed and his associates.

He continued to pick winners in the races, but the more successful he was the more Big Ed demanded. It wasn't only horses, but greyhound racing, followed by card games. Clive enjoyed poker for a time, but soon tired of the late nights and all the smoke-filled rooms. When he asked for an early night Big Ed would go into a rage, saying he had invested a lot of money in him and this was the thanks he got.

Clive decided never to ask for any more early nights. Instead, he continued to advise Big Ed without complaint. Charlie and Dino warned him that he was making a lot of enemies, for every time Big Ed won at poker, the rival gangs knew Clive was behind it.

One night, insect repellent was sprayed over a cheap novel Clive was given for supper. Clive became very ill after the first few pages. At first he thought it was because the book was so poorly written, but Dino spotted the can of spray hidden in a flowerpot nearby. Clive collapsed and was rushed back to Big Ed's mansion where he was unable to move or eat for several days.

He gave up eating books after that and snacked on magazines and tabloid newspapers. Soon he tired of reading altogether. Any spare time he had, he watched TV and fed on toilet rolls or kitchen paper. He began to feel more and more depressed.

He had no one to talk to except Big Ed and his gang, who spent all their time gambling or talking about money. No one talked about Keats or Shelley. Never a mention of Leonardo or Picasso. Only the usual smutty jokes, then they would end up laughing like hyenas. It was all becoming far too boring for Clive. Wilfred always used to say that one should learn something new every day, to keep one's brain stimulated. It was too much of an effort to read any more, except for the racing pages which he had to read. Big Ed said it was in his contract and he couldn't break it.

Things changed for the worse when Clive was brought to a big dinner party in honour of Big Ed. Clive had never seen such tough-looking customers in all his life. They were all saying wonderful things about Big Ed, but Clive felt their words were hollow and didn't ring true. Big Ed got up to thank all his business associates who had travelled great distances to honour him. Then he scooped Clive up with a silver teaspoon and proudly showed him off.

"I struck gold when I came across this little midget here. I mean 'bookworm'," he laughed heartily.

Charlie and Dino patted each other on the back. Their own luck had certainly improved since stealing Clive from that basement. They were a lot richer and wore fancy clothes.

Big Ed received a loud round of applause after his speech.

One man with oily hair and a pencil moustache leaned over to a heavyset man wearing dark glasses. "I lost over ten grand thanks to that slimy bug advising Big Ed during a poker classic."

"You want me to make a hit, boss?" asked the other man.

"After dessert."

"I'll squash him like the bug that he is," the heavyset man growled under his breath.

"Nothing too messy," ordered the other man, producing a gold pin from his lapel with a golden rose on top. "Say it with flowers," he sniggered.

When they had finished their coffee, the heavyset man stood up and headed towards where Big Ed and Clive were sitting. As the assassin passed close to Clive, he stuck the pin through the bookworm. Fortunately for Clive, he was a very small target and the man's aim wasn't good – the pin pierced Clive's tail. The injury looked worse than it was. Clive fainted from the shock. Nobody heard him over the loud jazz music which had started up after the speeches. The assassin returned to his seat.

"Well?" said the other man. "Did you get him?"

"He won't be giving Big Ed any more help," he said. "He's like a sausage on a cocktail stick."

Big Ed turned to say something to Clive but, to his horror, poor Clive lay still on the table, a sharp pin piercing his body. Big Ed shouted loudly. "Someone has taken out my little pet, and someone is going to pay!"

Suddenly all kinds of weapons were produced from pockets, trouser-legs, coats and hats. Then, to everyone's surprise, the doors of the restaurant were flung wide and a battalion of police rushed in. With battens raised high and whistles blowing, they hurried to arrest all the guests. Some tried to escape through the back door but found the police had surrounded the building.

In all the scuffle, the table where Clive was lying was knocked over, sending him and all its contents crashing to the floor.

Chapter 8

On the Streets Again

The following day Clive was swept up with all the damaged delph and food, dropped into a plastic bag, and put out the back door. Clive slowly came to with a terrible pain in his head and an even worse pain in his tail. Then he remembered what had happened. Try as he might, he could not remove the sharp pin from his body.

Suddenly there was movement outside the black refuse sack. He knew it wasn't a human, for the movement was much quieter than that. Then he heard the sound of tearing. A hole began to appear in the bag, then an amber eye peered in at him.

It was a wily city fox out on patrol looking for an easy meal. He was rewarded with half-eaten T-bone steaks and chicken legs. Clive tried to stay very still but the rest of the bag's contents spilled out on to the ground. The fox spotted Clive and stopped eating its steak to investigate.

"Good evening," said Clive. "I wouldn't bother with me," he continued. "I'm not very tasty. Besides, I have a nasty pin through my tail which would hurt your tongue."

The fox smiled. "It's okay, little fellow. You're not on the menu." He examined Clive's tail. "What happened to you?"

"It's a long and unpleasant story, Mr Fox."

"Call me Redser," said the fox.

"I'm Clive," said Clive. "I'm a bookworm."

"Would you like some steak?" asked the fox.

"No, thank you, a nice plain sheet of white paper is all I could manage."

"I'm afraid there's none of that around here," said the fox. "Listen, why don't I try to remove that pin from your body? It looks very uncomfortable."

"I would be most grateful if you could," said Clive.

The fox made several attempts to get a grip on the pin, without much luck. There was only one thing for it. He wedged Clive behind the prongs of a discarded fork and grabbed the pin with his teeth. This did the trick – the pin was removed in an instant.

Clive was most grateful to Redser.

"You take it easy and I'll get you some supper." The fox padded away. Clive rested on a head of lettuce; it was most comfortable. Luckily for him, bookworms heal very quickly and, by the time the fox returned, there was no trace of the hole made by the pin.

"I've brought you a newspaper. It's today's! Should still be crispy," smiled the fox.

Clive's eyes opened wide as he read the headlines:

"Public Enemy No 1 Big Ed Killalot was arrested by police after a raid on a very popular restaurant in the city centre last night. Full report on page three."

"So Big Ed was not only involved in gambling but in other nasty things," said Clive to himself. He was certainly glad to be rid of that lot.

"You can read?" said Redser.

"I can," said Clive. "Let me see, is there anything of interest in the paper for you?" The fox sat and waited. Clive turned the pages. "Ah yes, here's something you might find interesting:

"Fur coats make a welcome return in the autumn collections of New York, Paris and London fashion houses. Leopard, beaver, seal and fox prove the most popular among the rich . . . " Before he could finish, the fox gave a loud yelp, turned on his heels and hurried down the alleyway as if his tail was on fire.

"Oh, why did I have to open my big mouth," sighed Clive. "He was rather nice, I was enjoying his company. Oh, well, that seems to be the story of my life, losing friends." He picked up the pin, tore a few corners off the paper, impaled them on the pin, then put it over his shoulder. If he got hungry he could have a snack.

Under the light of the full moon he made his way slowly down the alleyway. Despite the fact that there was a cold wind blowing, Clive removed the suit Big Ed had made for him. He didn't want anything to remind him of that experience.

He spent the next few days inching along the streets, living off discarded newspapers and a few brown chip bags. The smell of vinegar reminded him of the good times he'd once had with Jodie, Jack and the others.

One evening he took a wrong turn and wandered into a laneway that was patrolled by a gang of tough-looking beetles. "This is our patch," said one of the angry gang. "Nobody comes in here without our permission. You dig?"

"Well, I don't dig, actually," said Clive. "I've never had any need to."

"Oh, a wise guy," said another. Suddenly six of them leaped on Clive and began to beat him up.

Luckily for him, a hedgehog came scurrying down the lane and sent the beetles scuttling away. The hedgehog sniffed Clive. "Are you all right?"

"Fine now, thanks to you."

"My name is Amy," said the hedgehog. "What's yours?"

"Clive," said Clive. "I'm a bookworm."

"Climb up on my back," suggested the hedgehog. "If you spread your weight evenly, the spines won't hurt you. I'll bring you some place safe."

Clive climbed up and lay down flat. It worked. It was rather comfortable, and reminded him of pictures he had seen of humans lying on a bed of nails in India.

The hedgehog hurried down the streets under the cover of darkness, keeping to the gardens and shadows. "It's quite shocking that a bookworm like yourself can't walk the streets without being bullied."

"I agree with you," said Clive. "If there's one thing I can't stand, it's violence. Why can't they take up a hobby or do something useful? Read some poetry, for instance."

"What?" asked Amy.

"Poetry. I'll bet you've never seen a poet beat up another person, have you?"

"No, I don't think so," said Amy, not sure what a poet was.

"You see," said Clive, "poets are too busy being creative."

"I'm sure you're right," said Amy. "You seem very intelligent."

Clive was pleased with himself. Someone actually agreed with him for a change.

"Well, this is where I live," said Amy,

indicating a small hole below the roots of a horse chestnut tree near a park.

Clive thanked her for the ride and made his way, inch by inch, towards the city centre. He loved the bright lights and the bustle of traffic. He enjoyed seeing people enjoying themselves – even if he wasn't. He crawled into a discarded can and slept soundly.

Chapter 9

All's Well That Ends Well

Early the next morning he headed for Trinity College. He had always wanted to see the Book of Kells and promised himself he wouldn't try to nibble it, no matter how tempting it was. He shouted hello to all the students hurrying to lectures, but none of them seemed to hear him.

He saw the sign pointing to the Book of Kells. There were a lot of visitors wandering about. Clive crawled up to the glass case that the book was kept in. He'd barely had a chance to take a peek when a large American tourist let out a loud shriek as she spotted Clive.

Various people tried to swot him as he made his way back to the floor.

"It wouldn't happen back in Ohio," said another American lady, trying to comfort the first.

The security man quickly spotted Clive and lifted him up on a lollipop stick, removing him from the premises. Clive was unceremoniously dumped on to a patch of grass outside the college.

Clive wished he was a normal bookworm again, instead of living this life of an outcast. He decided to crawl back into the college. No one was going to throw him out, not with his intellect. He would complain to the Provost about his ill-treatment.

Just then, he noticed an anxious-looking student. "You look worried," said Clive.

The student answered, as if talking to himself, "I wish I didn't have to sit this exam . . ."

"W h o didn't do his s t u d y i n g, then?" said Clive.

"It's true," admitted the student. "I

suppose I should have spent more time studying than playing rugby."

"I understand," said Clive. "I really do. Not that I've ever played rugby – far too rough for me." Then Clive had an idea. He crawled up the student's back, over his shoulder, and slipped into his shirt pocket.

"I must be going bonkers," said the student. "Talking to myself and my brain answering in a different voice." He took a deep breath and walked in to sit the exam.

Nervously he picked up his pen and read the exam paper that was passed around by the examiner. He took a big gulp as he read the first question. The second was even worse. As he scanned the pages, each question seemed impossible for him to answer. He looked around – all the other students were busy writing. Then he heard the small voice in his ear again: "Just relax and begin with the first question." As the student looked at the question, the answer suddenly popped into his head like magic. The student quickly wrote it down. It certainly seemed right as he read over it again. Then the voice gave him the answer to the next question, and the next. He quickly wrote them down.

Before long, he had finished answering all the questions. He was so pleased with himself that he gave out a loud yelp. The examiner looked over his glasses disapprovingly. The student was so relieved he almost danced out of the exam hall.

Clive chuckled to himself. He was glad he'd helped the student out. For his reward he treated himself to a square of chocolate from a bar in the student's pocket.

As the student passed by a cherry tree Clive decided to take his leave. He climbed on to the student's shoulder, caught hold of one of the twiglets, and swung on to it. He clung to the branch watching the students passing by, some racing to class, others holding hands. As he watched, he was reminded of love poems he had read.

He began to recite one of Shakespeare's sonnets . . . "Love's not Time's fool, though rosy lips and cheeks . . ."

"That's lovely," said a voice from above. Looking up, Clive found himself face to face with the most beautiful lady butterfly. She glided down beside him.

"You're a painted lady," he said in awe.

"You're cute," said the butterfly. Clive's glasses began to steam up and he started to blush. "That was lovely, what you said earlier," she said softly, fanning him with her delicate wings.

"It's a sonnet written by William Shakespeare, born in Stratford-upon-Avon on April 23rd 1554 and died in 1616 on his birthday."

"Very impressive," said the butterfly. Clive blushed again. "It's unusual to see a bookworm up a tree," she remarked.

Clive explained that he had once lived in a lovely old library and what had happened when they began to refurbish it. He told her about meeting two dear friends called Jack and Bernard in a café called the Honey Pot.

"I know that place," said the butterfly. "I've passed it many a time on my way to the park."

"You do?" said Clive excitedly.

"I can take you there," said the butterfly. "But first, you must tell me your name."

"I'm Clive," said Clive, blushing again.

"Then call me Monica," she said tenderly. "Climb aboard," she offered. Clive climbed up. "Hold on tight! I don't want you falling off." Clive hugged her tightly and his glasses steamed up again.

She flapped away, floating in the air like a leaf over the college. Up Grafton Street, across St Stephens Green they went, Clive was really enjoying the flight and such beautiful company. On and on they floated. until she began to hover in the air. There, just below, Clive could see the sign for the Honey Pot, except it looked a bit different – as if it had been redecorated.

Reading out the newspaper crossword, Jack said "What is a ha-ha?"

Bernard stroked his chin. "A laugh, of course."

"No, that doesn't fit." Jack scratched his head.

"It's a sunken boundary wall, a device used to have an unobstructed view beyond a garden."

"That's it," said Jack.

"It wasn't me," said Bernard.

"No?" said Jack. "Then who was it?"

Just then, a butterfly alighted on the counter between the two men and Clive climbed down. "Good-day, gentlemen."

The two men couldn't believe their eyes. "Clive, you're back!" said Jack. "I could hug you only I'm afraid I might squash you."

Clive introduced Monica.

"Is she your lady friend?" asked Bernard.

Clive blushed. "No, we've just met."

"Just good friends," laughed Jack.

Bernard picked up the phone and called Jodie. "Jodie, come to the café at once. Clive's back!" Then he rang Rita, who was out in the back garden reading. Rita shrieked with joy when she heard the news.

It wasn't long before Jodie and Rita hurried in through the front door.

"Where is he, where is he?" they both asked in unison.

Bernard pointed to the counter with a big smile on his face and, when Jodie looked down and saw Clive, she couldn't believe her eyes. Scooping  him up gently, she stroked his head. "Welcome back," she said tenderly. "We thought we had lost you for good."

Clive introduced Monica. "She's a painted lady," he said.

"Still full of information," smiled Jodie.

They all decided to go for lunch. Clive tucked in to some paper napkins while Monica was content to take some nectar from the flower on the table. Then, to Clive's amazement, he spotted Wilfred on top of the bowler hat of a man who had just arrived into the restaurant.

"Wilfred!" Clive shouted excitedly.

"Clive!" Wilfred exclaimed.

The man removed his hat and hung it on a hatstand. He looked over at Bernard. "My name is Godfrey, actually."

"I don't believe it," said Clive.

"I don't care whether you do or not," said the man. "But my name is Godfrey. I don't know any Wilfreds or Clives."

Jack and Bernard broke into hoots of laughter.

"I think I'll take my custom elsewhere," said the man, putting back on his bowler hat and turning to leave.

"Jump!" Clive shouted to Wilfred.

It seemed a long way down, thought Wilfred, but it was now or never. "Geronimo!" he yelled as he jumped off the hat.

Jodie held out her hands and caught him.

The man with the bowler hat turned back once again before he left. "For the last time, my name is Godfrey, not Wilfred, Clive *or* Geronimo!" Then, turning, he slammed the restaurant door behind him as he left.

After they had all recovered from the

laughter, Jack turned to the older bookworm with the grey whiskers. "So you're the famous Wilfred!"

"Oh, I wouldn't say that at all," Wilfred blushed with embarrassment.

"You taught Clive well," said Jodie. "He says you were his mentor."

"Oh, goodness me, no. All I ever tried to do was instil a love of books."

Clive smiled awkwardly and said he hadn't read a book for months.

"Oh, we'll have to remedy that," said Wilfred. Then he admitted that he too had fallen on hard times and hadn't seen a book or a library for over a year.

"Well, your luck is about to change," said Rita. "You may not have heard, but I won the Lottery. Me, who never won even a box of chocolates before!"

"So that's why the Honey Pot looks so splendid," said Clive.

"Thank you," said Bernard and Rita.

Then a handsome young man appeared at the table. "This is Richard, my boyfriend," said Jodie. "He's in the music business." Richard looked somewhat surprised to see two bookworms and a butterfly sitting on the table. "I've made my first CD, thanks to Richard here." She squeezed his hand.

"It's in the charts already at number eighteen and rising," said Richard proudly.

Clive was thrilled for Jodie.

Then Rita said, "Now, your surprise." Clive looked blank. The others had a knowing expression on their faces.

"I'm completely in the dark," admitted Clive.

"Well, it's like this," said Jodie. "Since Rita here has won the Lottery – and as she has such a big heart – she's agreed to open a new children's library in the local school."

"Oh, the one we did the table quiz for?" said Clive, remembering.

"The very same one. And I know the school would be honoured if you helped them to choose suitable books and file and log them. Whatever librarians do . . ." said Rita.

"I'm speechless," said Clive. "It's a dream come true . . ."

"There are two conditions," said Rita.

"What are they?" enquired Clive.

"You must ask Wilfred to assist you."

"I would be delighted to," said Wilfred, embracing Clive. "I simply love young people's literature."

"And the other is," she paused and wiped her lips with a napkin while Clive looked on anxiously, "no eating the books," she said. "The

school principal is very insistent on that."

"Fear not," said Clive. "From now on I'm turning over a new leaf. I'll eat only paper napkins and the occasional plate of chips!"

They all laughed loudly.